CITY OF DREAMS

ADVENTURES IN THE UNDERWORLD

GERALDINE MCCAUGHREAN
ILLUSTRATED BY TONY ROSS

ORCHARD BOOKS

CITY OF DREAMS

Aeneas dreamed that a woman's voice was telling him to wake up, and he woke to the sound of buildings falling. There was fire too – a throaty roar like a wild beast eating up Troy. Aeneas knew instantly that the Greeks were inside the city. After ten years of fruitless siege, they had finally found a way in.

Opening the door on to the night, he found the streets bright as day with fire, Greek warriors meting out death to every Trojan man, woman and child. He had to get his family away!

Running through the smoke-filled rooms, he caught his young son Iulus by the hand, heaved his old father on to his back, and ran for the harbour, shouting for his household and servants to follow.

Not until he reached the waterfront did he realise that his wife was missing, and start back to find her.

He glimpsed her, too, paler than pale, waving to him from an upper window, beyond a curtain of fire. "I am dead, Aeneas!" called her lovely ghost. "Another bride is waiting for you – I will send her to wait for you – on the river bank…!"

Then she was gone. A tower crashed to the ground. The whole city of Troy shivered and sobbed, and the doors of burning buildings slammed like a dozen drumbeats, out of time. Snatching up a burning baulk of timber, Aeneas carried it back to the ship – a piece of Troy, a piece of Troy burning. It seemed important.

8

Standing at the mast of his ship, his servants grunting and straining at the oars, Aeneas peered astern through the pall of smoke. It seemed to him that figures larger than mere men were beating down the high, white walls of Troy: giant men and women cloaked in light were crazing the palisades with mallets of gold, leaning their shoulders against her towers, breathing fire over the city of his birth.

"What do you see, son?" asked his father, eyes too old for visions.

"The gods themselves," breathed Aeneas, "siding with the Greeks to destroy us!"

Anchises nodded his grizzled head. "Yes, yes. Your mother always said it was Troy's destiny to fall."

"My mother?"

But Anchises would say no more. He never had told, nor ever could tell Aeneas the identity of his mother. Had he not sworn on his life to keep it secret?

Aeneas got away; his destiny demanded
it. He sailed to Crete, thinking it was as
good a home as any, for a man made
homeless. But once landed and asleep on
the shores of Crete, he dreamed the most
extraordinary dream of his life.

He dreamed that he stood in his house once more, surrounded by the statues of his household gods. "Seek out the land of Italy, Aeneas," their stone mouths seemed to be saying.

"There you shall found an empire greater even than Greece or Troy, its feet standing in Africa, its hands reaching into the lands of snow. The great, straight highways of the world shall be its arteries! One day, a city greater than Troy shall sit on seven hills, and the smoke from its altars rise up to Heaven. Such is the will of the gods!"

Aeneas woke, and lay awake till morning, watching the sparks from the burning Trojan brand spiral upwards towards the stars. Then, at first light, he told his family and servants to reboard the ship.

Again he asked Anchises, "Who was my mother? Did she die when I was born? Why don't I remember her? Why have I never seen her? Why won't you tell me...?" But the old man only put a finger to his lips. As Aeneas carried his father aboard, Anchises hung like a sick sheep around a shepherd's shoulders. Every day he was growing weaker.

Wading home from Troy, the gods brushed the ashes and stone dust from their robes and watched the little ships coming and going over the surface of the sea like the pieces of a board game.

"I see a Trojan left alive!" said Juno. "Does he think he can escape the fate ordained for Troy and all its princes?" And she went to the Keeper of the Winds and borrowed his leather sack. Loosing its cords, she freed them all: the north and south, the east and west winds to roll up the ocean and shake it like a rug.

Aeneas's ship was beaten by blue clods of water large as hills. Shoals of fish, a debris of dolphins and octopuses and turtles rained down on the rowers, while

wrecks from the sea bed came spinning
by. Iulus clung to his father in terror.

"Hush, child, hush," said Aeneas. "I
was born to die a dry death." Even so, the
sea was pouring in over the stern, filling
the hull, driving the whole vessel under...

Just then, Neptune, god of the sea, woken by the huge upheaval in his bed, thrust his bleary head out of the water to find waterspouts gumming together sea and sky, and everywhere whirlpools dimpling the sea.

"*Cease! Be still! Who has been meddling in my domain?*" Then he smoothed flat the sea with his great green hands.

Seeing Aeneas's ship foundering, he raised it to the surface once again, the water gushing out of its bilges, the little Trojan flame still glimmering at its masthead. *"While the seas are mine, only I shall sink ships!"* the god declared, catching the winds like flies between his palms.

The storm had driven them so far off course that they had no idea where they were. But, sighting land, Aeneas and his crew pulled for the shore, where they offered up thanks to the gods for sparing them. Old Anchises, though, was chilled to the bone. Though the light of the campfire glimmered in his eyes, it had no power to warm him.

"Live a little longer, Father!" begged Aeneas. "If the gods are willing, you and I will reach Italy and begin a new life!"

Anchises only smiled sadly. "Your mother will stay by you. She will see you safely to your destiny. My time is over."

"My mother? What do you mean?" said Aeneas.

Anchises shut his eyes. "I don't doubt she loves you as much as I do… Is she not Love itself, after all? Venus. The goddess Venus." And having broken his promise, Anchises breathed out his last breath, and died, leaving his son, weeping and amazed, on the shores of Libya, beneath the walls of Carthage.

ADVENTURES IN THE UNDERWORLD

The son of Venus! The son of the goddess of love! Little wonder, then, that Aeneas fell in love with Queen Dido the moment they met. Ruler of the sumptuous city of Carthage, Dido was as beautiful as the snowy Atlas peaks. One sight of her, and Aeneas forgot his grief, forgot his dreams, forgot where he was going.

"O mother Venus!" prayed Aeneas,
"if ever you cared for this mortal heart
of mine, grant me the love of this Queen!"

On the slopes of Olympus Venus sighed
a sentimental sigh. How could she refuse
her own dear son? Clapping her hands, she
summoned her other, immortal son, the
boy Cupid.

"Go there, dear child, and aim true.
No mistakes now! This concerns my son's
happiness. So aim your arrows straight
and true."

Cupid did better. Speeding down to earth, he nestled close to Dido (who was fond of children, and mistook him for an ordinary boy). Taking one of his arrows in his chubby little fist, he anointed it with the venom called Love...and drove it deep into Dido's heart.

As deep as the worst of arrow wounds, Love invaded the Queen of Carthage. She lost all interest in affairs of state. Aeneas lost all thought of journeying further. His household servants, kicking their heels unhappily about the spacious courts and gardens of Carthage, asked each other, "When are we going to set sail? When will he tear himself away?" And Jupiter, watching from Olympus, drummed his fingers impatiently on the parapets of Heaven: "*Does he not know he is keeping history waiting?*" and sent his messenger Mercury down to Carthage.

Mercury, on his winged heels, went scudding downwards, carefully carrying a clutch of dreams, which he broke over Aeneas's pillow.

"You have forgotten!"

"No time to waste!"

"The unborn are waiting for you!"

"Ask the Sibyl!"

"Ask the way!"

The dreams harangued Aeneas until he woke with his hands over his ears, heart pounding. Yes, he had abandoned his mission for the sake of his own selfish happiness! Aeneas leapt out of bed. There was no time to lose. Love was sweet, but what of Duty? What of Destiny? His heart yearned after Dido like a little boat tugging at its anchor chain, but he tore himself free and set sail. Queen Dido woke in time to see the mast, with its smoking Trojan brand, dip below the horizon.

She had no 'Duty' to solace her. She had no dreams, no gods whispering in her ear. She had made Aeneas her god and worshipped him day and night. Now he was gone.

"Gather up every shirt he wore, every sheet he ever slept on," she told her servants, "every plate he ate off, every chariot he ever drove!" Her face was a mask of hatred. Dido had all Aeneas's possessions piled up in a bonfire and set alight. Her face was a picture of fury.

Now she will forget him, thought her suitors and courtiers. Now she will spit on his memory and forget false, lying Aeneas – and good riddance!

"He abandoned you."
"He jilted you."
"He deceived you," they agreed, smugly sympathising with their Queen.

"He is gone," she said, and the look of hatred melted, gave way to grief. She could pretend no longer to hate Aeneas.

Leaping into the bonfire, she drew a dagger and plunged it into her own breast. It entered through the very wound Cupid's arrow had made, and she died within the space of a single word: *"Aeneas!"*

The Sibyl of Cumae knew much about the future of the world. All day she sat in her cave, on the edge of a vast, trackless forest, writing down prophecies, page after page, volume after volume. Already she knew how Aeneas would avoid the whirlpool Charybdis, the Clashing Rocks, the monsters of the deep sea.

But she was also wise enough to see
what stood in front of her: an unhappy
man, listless and dull-eyed, wishing he
were back in Carthage.

"The man who plucks the golden bough
Is he alone the gods allow
To go where no soul else draws breath:
To trespass in the Realm of Death."

That shook Aeneas out of his
melancholy. "Hades, you mean? The
Underworld? I don't want to go to Hades!
Soon enough when I'm dead! Visit the

spirits, you mean? How? Why?" He was appalled. "I won't do it!" But he was also intrigued. "How do I find this golden branch? One branch in a forest of this size?"

At that very moment, a small white dove fluttered into the Sibyl's cave and settled on Aeneas's shoulder. Its wing brushed his ear; it pressed its plump breast against his cheek and crooned to him. Then it flew off between the trees. And in that disguise, Venus led her son through the dark, primeval woods which smother the Cumaean countryside.

At the end of the thousandth path, in the darkest heart of the sunless wood, a giant ball of mistletoe glowed like a setting sun. It had no root, as the trees around it had roots, but clung to an oak, drawing its nourishment from the tree as a bat sucks blood.

Climbing up to pick it, climbing down armed with this golden bough, Aeneas ran back to his ship. He set course for Ocean River which flows over the edge of the world. His voyage was lit by twin brands: the Trojan flame and the golden mistletoe.

The darkness grew so dense, so solid that his ship ran aground on it, and he had to continue on foot. Through the Cave of Sleep and Death he passed, where the two giants, Mors and Somnus slept, their poppy crowns askew. In the corners of the room, invisible but for the whites of their rolling eyes, lurked nightmares. A feathery rustling overhead told of sweeter dreams roosting in the eaves.

Now and then, a dream or nightmare would dash out through one of two doors – one of ivory, the other of stone: dreams that would come true; dreams to trick and mislead the dreamer. The air of the cave was darkly peppered with seeds from the poppies, and it was all Aeneas could do to stifle his yawns and keep his lids from closing.

The giant Mors slept deepest of all, of course, for his was the sleep of Death.

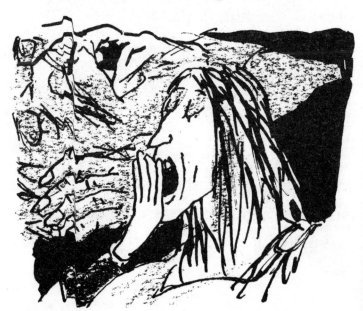

Beyond the Cave of Sleep lay the River
Lethe and its solitary ferryboat, the glaring
ferryman demanding his fare from spirits
newly arrived. At the sight of Aeneas and
the golden bough, however, they fell back,
like wolves from a burning brand.

Aeneas rode the ferry across Lethe,
and the guard dog, three-headed Cerberus
tamely let him pass into the Underworld,
gazing moon-eyed with all its snarling heads.

That is how Aeneas came to meet with his dead wife once more; with old friends whose adventures had carried them over the brink; with his old father Anchises.

"I have been waiting for you, my son," Anchises said, no longer old, yet not young either; his face empty of either smiles or sorrow.

He led Aeneas down clammy tunnels to the door of a cavern quite unlike the rest. "This is the Hall of Unborn Souls,"

he said, spreading wide his arms. "For fear you turn back, let me show you the people who are relying on you to succeed in your adventure."

The whole cavern shimmered with light from a thousand standing pools. In every pool, shining bright as goldfish, swam restless shreds of life.

"Look. Here are Romulus and Remus; brave Camillus; the world-conquering Caesars. There is Portia, Horatius Cocles, Philemon and Baucis the priests, see? And there! Marcus Curtius. Look!  The mighty Augustus – and Virgil the poet, there! Coriolanus the General and Tarquin the Proud." Anchises gave a small shiver. "Some good, some bad, some the stuff of legend. Will you leave them here, in this everlasting dark of Unbeing? Unborn? Nameless? No more than dreams in the mind of the gods?"

"No! Never!" cried Aeneas. Gathering his cloak around him, he asked a blessing from his father's ghost, shouted a farewell to the million watching ghosts, begged forgiveness from Jupiter for wasting so much time, and help from winged Mercury to speed him on his way. Then he left Hades as fast as any galloping nightmare, and returned to his ship more afire than even the golden bough in his hand.

"Onwards, men! To Italy! Row for the mouth of the Tiber! There is work to be done!"

Sailing up the Tiber from the sea, Aeneas
found green banks where wild grapes
grew, forests noisy with boar, glades
ghostly with pale deer.

Urging his oarsmen higher and higher
upstream, he saw at last a red-haired girl
sitting on the bank, who lifted her head

and watched the ship with curious eyes. Though she had come there to fish, she had the air of someone waiting. The words of his ghostly wife echoed softly through his brain: *"Another bride is waiting for you – I will send her to wait for you – on the river bank...!"*

"What place is this?" called
Aeneas, but she did not understand
him. A different language. Another race.
Finally, by signs and gestures, they made
her understand, and she called back:
"*Latium. Ecce Latium.*"

Since this was to be his home, the first thing Aeneas had to do was build an altar to Vesta, goddess of hearth and home. The one he raised that evening was no more than a crude pile of stones, but it would have to do. The temple could follow later. Piling the cairn with flowers and branches, Aeneas set them burning with the torch he had carried out of Troy.

"Let this flame never go out!" he told his companions. Let it be tended night and day, for this is the flame of the Past which will light our way to the Future."

On the shrine to Vesta, the golden spray of mistletoe burned with a lively, popping crackle and a bitter-sweet smell.